Disney · PIXAR

TOY STORY

Ride 'em, Cowboy!

For Vincent Cavaniola

—K.M.

This is for Quim, Liesel, Edgar, Neysa Bove, and Marcos Guerra,
who give me the most support, encouragement, and of course…inspiration.

—L.B.

Book design by Winnie Ho

Copyright © 2009 Disney Enterprises, Inc./Pixar. Based on characters from the motion pictures *Toy Story* Copyright © 1995 Disney Enterprises, Inc. and *Toy Story 2* Copyright © 1999 Disney Enterprises, Inc./Pixar. Original *Toy Story* elements © Disney Enterprises, Inc. Etch A Sketch®© The Ohio Art Company. Slinky® Dog © Poof-Slinky.

Printed in the United States of America
First Edition
3 5 7 9 10 8 6 4 2
ILS NO: F322-836800/274 2009
Library of Congress Cataloging-in-Publication Data on file.
ISBN 978-1-4231-1056-9
Visit www.disneybooks.com

Ride 'em, Cowboy!

by Kate McMullan

Illustrated by Lorelay Bove

Disney PRESS

New York

Cowboy Bob *rode the bull for eight seconds,*
Andy read to his toys. *Cowboy Bob won the Silver Buckle.*
He was the rodeo champ!

"Andy!" called his mom. "Into the car, or we'll be late
for the rodeo."

"**Yee-haw!**" yelled Andy, and he raced from the room.

A **rodeo** . . . thought Woody. Why not?

"Rodeo time!" yelled Woody.

"Yahoo!" cried Jessie. "I'm the fastest rope in the West!"

"Oh, right," said Woody. "Let me show you how to rope a wild bronco."

"You mean a wild Bronco-*saurus*,"
said Hamm.

Rex grinned. "Who, *me*?"

"**Watch this!**" hollered Jessie.

"Triple play!" Jessie grinned. "Got the whole flock."

"Lucky ropin', cowgirl," said Woody. "But I'm the rodeo champ around these parts."

"Well, now . . ." said Jessie. "Care to pit your skills against mine, cowboy?"
"You're on!" said Woody.

"Aw right!" cried Slinky Dog. "We're havin' a rodeo!"
"Let's get organized!" called Buzz.

"Rodeo ring right here." Buzz pointed. "Chute over there."

"I want to be in the rodeo!" said Rex.

"Ready!" announced Buzz. "First event—steer wrestling!"

"I'll be a steer!" called Rex.

"We've got it covered, Rex," said Buzz. "Hamm?"

"On it!" said Hamm.

"Uh . . . how 'bout a practice run?" said Woody.

"Don't worry, Woody," coached Slinky Dog. "Just take him down fast."

"Go!" called Buzz.

"Yee-haw!" cried Woody as he and Bullseye burst out of the chute.

"Moooo!" said Hamm. "I say, moo!" He jumped on a skate.

Hamm sped away from Woody. He hit a log and it went flying.
"Look out, Woody!" yelled Slinky.

"Bullseye—jump!" cried Woody.

Bullseye leaped over the log and galloped closer to the "steer."

Woody sprang off his horse and onto Hamm. He tried to wrestle him to the ground.

"Give it up, Woody," said Hamm. "I'm packin' twelve-fifty in quarters."

"Uhhhh," Woody groaned.

Next it was Jessie's turn. She whistled for Bullseye and jumped on his back. "Yee-haw!" she cried, galloping after the steer.

"**What, again?**" cried Hamm, and he took off running. Bullseye caught up with Hamm.

Jessie jumped onto Hamm's back. She held on to his change slot with one hand and tickled his belly with the other. **"Kitchy-kitchy-koo!"** she cried.

"Hoo-hoo-hah!" Hamm laughed.
He rolled onto his side. **"Hoo-hoo! That tickles!"**

Jessie quickly
tied up Hamm.
Hamm stopped
laughing. "**Hey!**
No one told me
about this part of
the deal."

"I'm so glad I
wasn't the steer!"
said Rex.

"Nice wrestlin', little lady," said Buzz.
"What do you say now, Woody?" asked Jessie.
"Aw, I wasn't warmed up yet," said Woody.
"For cryin' out loud, **untie me!**" squealed Hamm.

"Barrel racing's next!" said Buzz. **"Barrels?"**
The Little Green Aliens lined up.
"Jessie? You're first," called Buzz. "Go!"
Jessie rode into the ring. She guided Bullseye around the barrels and back again without knocking any of them over.
"Fourteen seconds!" cried Buzz.

"Beat that, cowboy," said Jessie.

"Watch me, cowgirl," said Woody as he mounted his horse.

"Not too fast, Woody," warned Slinky.

"Go!" called Buzz.

"Ride like the wind, Bullseye!" cried Woody. Bullseye galloped for the barrels. **"Ooooooooh!"** cried the aliens.

"Faster, Bullseye!" shouted Woody. "We have to win!" Bullseye galloped faster.

"Oooooooh!" The aliens hunkered down and shut their eyes.

But Bullseye whizzed past them and galloped out the door.

"Aw, great!" said Slinky Dog. **"Just great!"**

"The winner is **Jessie!**" announced Buzz.

"Yay!" cheered the toys.

"Thanks a lot, Bullseye," muttered Woody.

"Last event—bull riding!" said Buzz.
"Sarge? Call the bull!"
"Sir! Yes, sir!" said Sarge. He whistled.
Buster nosed open the door and ran into Andy's room.
"Bull reporting for duty, sir!" Sarge added.

"Think you can ride that bull for eight seconds, cowboy?" asked Jessie.
"Nothin' to it, cowgirl," said Woody.

"**Rex?**" called Buzz. "You want to be the rodeo clown?"

"Yes! Absolutely!" cried Rex. "But—how do I make balloon animals with my little arms?"

"No balloons," said Buzz. "If Woody gets thrown, your job is to keep the bull busy till he gets up."

"Don't worry, Rex," said Woody. "I'm *not* getting thrown!"

Woody climbed
onto Buster's back.
"Hey, finger paints!"
said Rex. "I'll make
myself a clown suit!"
"Rex, shhhhh!" said
Buzz. "Woody? Go!"

Buster jumped out of the chute and ran around the ring.
"Ride 'em, cowboy!" yelled Slinky.
"Hey, Jessie!" cried Woody. "Watch *this!*"
And he stood up on Buster's back.

**"Sit down,
Woody!"** cried
Slinky.
Woody began
to wobble.

"Ahhhhhhh!"

Woody cried as he flew off
Buster's back.
    "To infinity and beyond!"
called Buzz.

SPLAT!

Woody hit the wall and slid down.

Slinky Dog ran over.

"You okay, Woody?"

"Yeahhhhh," said Woody.

"Next rider!" called Buzz.
"Yeeeeee-haaaaa!" yelled Jessie.

She held tight as
Buster bucked and
kicked and raced
around Andy's room.

"Eight seconds
are up!" said Buzz.
"We have our
rodeo champ!"

"**For a prize?**" said Buzz. "I'd—uh—like
you to have my Star Command belt buckle."

"Thanks a heap, spaceman!"
exclaimed Jessie.

Buzz grinned. "Etch?" he called.
"Get blazin' for the closing campfire!"

Woody caught up with Jessie on her way to the campfire.

"Well, you beat me fair and square, cowgirl," he said.

"This time, cowboy," said Jessie. "But there's always next time."

Woody sat down—very slowly.
"Where does it hurt?" asked Jessie.
"Everywhere," said Woody.

"To the tune of 'Home on the Range'!" cried Buzz. **"Sing it!"**

All the toys sang:

If you've got a rope,
And a heart full of hope,
And a horse that won't gallop away!
Get some boots and a hat,
If you've got all of that,
Then you'll be a cowpoke someday!

"Listen," said Buzz as the
song ended. "Footsteps!"
"Andy's home!" called
Woody. "Places!"

Seconds later, Andy galloped into his room.
He grabbed Woody and Jessie. **"Rodeo time!"** he
cried. "Which one of you is gonna be the rodeo champ?"

You know, it doesn't matter who's champ, thought Woody. It's all about having fun with the other cowpokes. **Yee-haw!**

RODEO: A contest in which cowboys and cowgirls show how good they are at taking care of cattle. If a calf on a ranch gets sick, a cowboy or cowgirl has to rope it, tie it down, and hold it still so the vet can examine it. In a rodeo, these skills are shown off in the tie-down roping event. Other exciting rodeo events are:

STEER WRESTLING or BULLDOGGING:
A steer is a male cow with long, sharp horns. In steer wrestling, a cowboy jumps off his horse onto a steer. He grabs it by the horns and "wrestles" it to the ground. The cowboy who does this the fastest is the winner. A winning time might be three or four seconds.

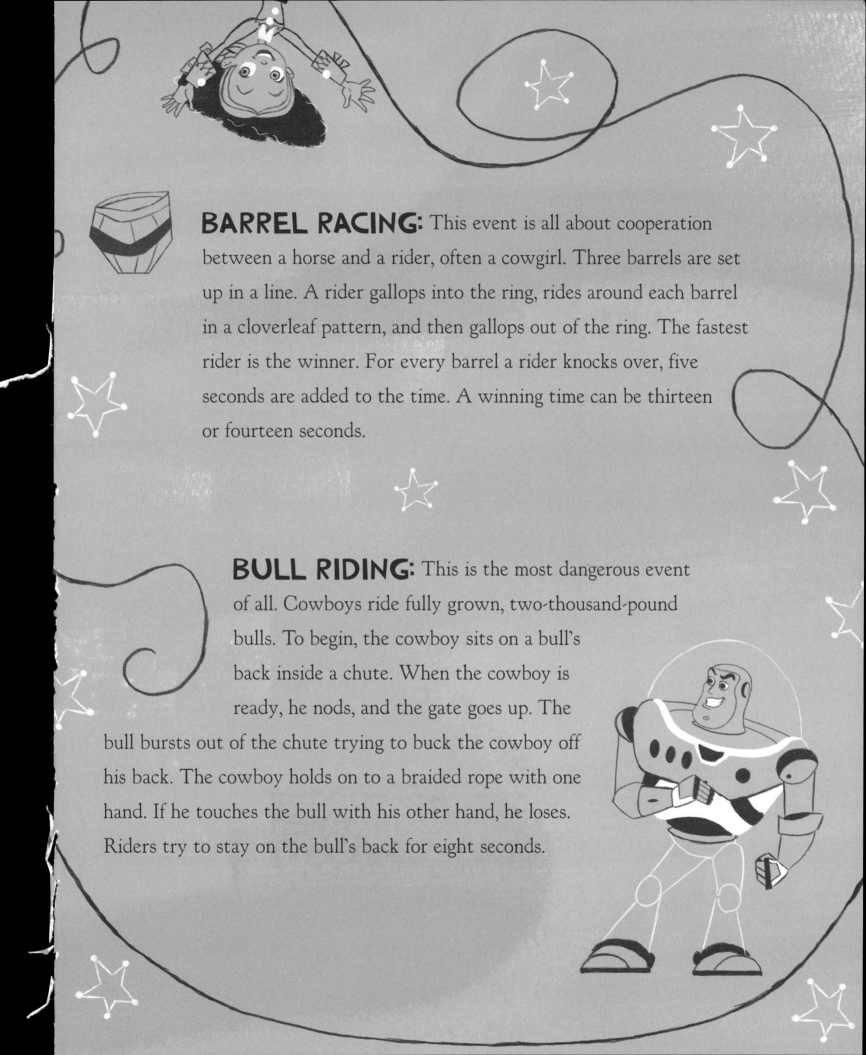

BARREL RACING: This event is all about cooperation between a horse and a rider, often a cowgirl. Three barrels are set up in a line. A rider gallops into the ring, rides around each barrel in a cloverleaf pattern, and then gallops out of the ring. The fastest rider is the winner. For every barrel a rider knocks over, five seconds are added to the time. A winning time can be thirteen or fourteen seconds.

BULL RIDING: This is the most dangerous event of all. Cowboys ride fully grown, two-thousand-pound bulls. To begin, the cowboy sits on a bull's back inside a chute. When the cowboy is ready, he nods, and the gate goes up. The bull bursts out of the chute trying to buck the cowboy off his back. The cowboy holds on to a braided rope with one hand. If he touches the bull with his other hand, he loses. Riders try to stay on the bull's back for eight seconds.

To my husband – Thank you for encouraging me to make this dream a reality. I couldn't have done it without your love and support.

To my nieces – Never stop reading, and never stop believing. Your dreams can really come true with enough faith, dedication, and hard work.

To the pup who inspired it all – **Rosie,** you are my constant companion, my fluffy pup, and my traveling piece of home. I never knew a six-pound fluffball could bring my life so much joy.

www.mascotbooks.com

The Princess Puppy

For more information, please contact:
Mascot Books
620 Herndon Parkway, Suite 320
Herndon, VA 20170
info@mascotbooks.com

Library of Congress Control Number: 2020906215

CPSIA Code: PRTWP0720A
ISBN-13: 978-1-64543-376-7

Printed in South Korea

The Princess

PUPPY

Kristin Sponaugle
Illustrated by Nidhom

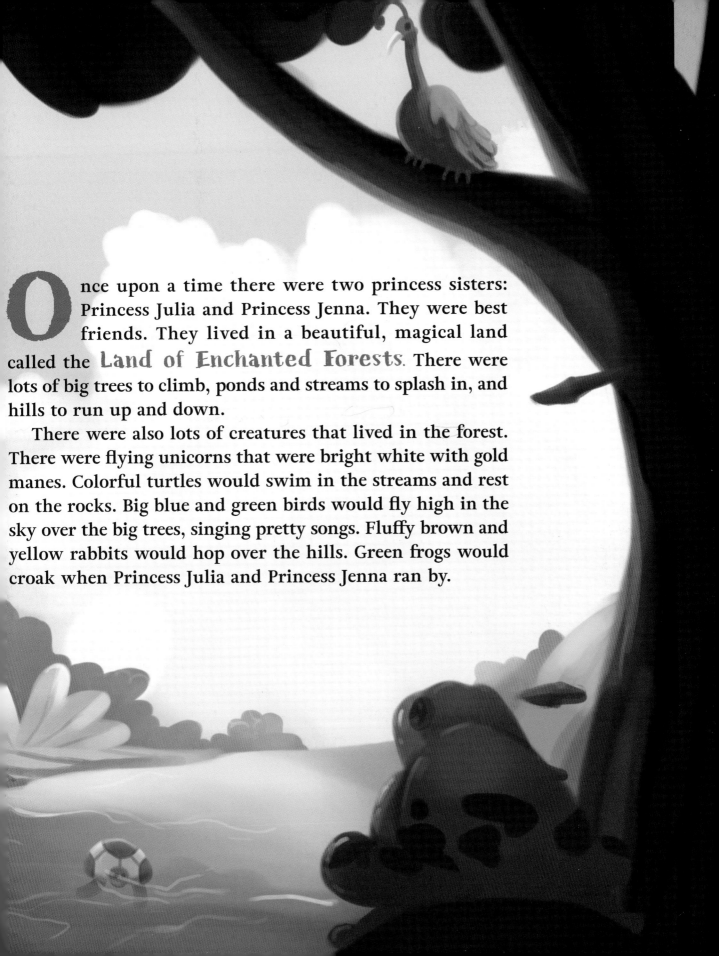

Once upon a time there were two princess sisters: Princess Julia and Princess Jenna. They were best friends. They lived in a beautiful, magical land called the Land of Enchanted Forests. There were lots of big trees to climb, ponds and streams to splash in, and hills to run up and down.

There were also lots of creatures that lived in the forest. There were flying unicorns that were bright white with gold manes. Colorful turtles would swim in the streams and rest on the rocks. Big blue and green birds would fly high in the sky over the big trees, singing pretty songs. Fluffy brown and yellow rabbits would hop over the hills. Green frogs would croak when Princess Julia and Princess Jenna ran by.

The two princesses loved playing outside. They would play hide-and-go-seek and hopscotch and see who could try to climb the highest tree. After a long day, the princess sisters would run inside their castle to have dinner with their mommy and daddy, the Queen and King of the Land of Enchanted Forests. Sometimes they ate things they didn't like, like lima beans. But mostly they ate yummy food, like macaroni.

Every night before bedtime, their parents would read them a story, tuck them in their beds, and kiss them good night. Princess Julia and Princess Jenna shared a room and sometimes would stay up after bedtime, giggling and whispering about their wonderful day outside.

One day, Princess Julia and Princess Jenna were laughing and running past all kinds of beautiful flowers in the big forest. Princess Julia yelled, "Catch me if you can!" and sprinted ahead. Princess Jenna started to run after her, but stopped when she saw a ball of white fluff sticking out of the bright red and yellow roses.

"Wait, Julia! Come look at this!" Princess Jenna called after her. Princess Jenna walked slowly toward the white fluffball. Suddenly, the white fluffball poked its head up through the flowers! Princess Jenna jumped back and knocked into her sister. "Oh my!" said Princess Julia. "What do you think that is?" The princesses had never seen a creature like this before!

Princess Jenna put her hand out to the small, trembling creature. "There, there, don't be scared. We won't hurt you," she whispered. "We just want to help you and be your friend." The animal cautiously sniffed her hand, then gently licked it. "Oh!" Jenna exclaimed. "That feels warm and tickles!"

Princess Julia said, "Look, she has on a pink collar. I think we should take her back to the castle to show Mommy and Daddy. They will probably know what she is." Princess Jenna gently picked up the fluffy creature and carried her back to the castle.

"**Mommy! Daddy!** Come here quick! Look what Jenna and I found in the forest!" Princess Julia cried as they entered the castle. "What is it, honey?" the Queen asked. Princess Jenna stepped forward and showed her mommy what was in her arms.

"I found her in the forest, hiding in the red and yellow roses. She seemed awfully scared but I think she's calmed down now," Princess Jenna said.

"Oh my," said the Queen. 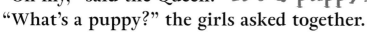 "It's a puppy!"

"What's a puppy?" the girls asked together.

"A puppy is a young dog, and a dog is a friendly, four-legged animal that comes from a very far-away place called the Land of Sunshine Mountains. Dogs usually live with people who take care of them. They wear collars so you can know their names and how to get ahold of their owners. This collar doesn't have anything written on it, though. I wonder how this puppy made it all the way to the Land of Enchanted Forests!" said the Queen.

"What should we do with her?" asked Princess Julia. "Can we keep her? Surely we can't expect her to survive outside in the forest!"

"No, this little puppy definitely can't stay outside," said the Queen with a sigh. "We'll keep her and she can be your pet." The Queen looked at both of her daughters. "You are both responsible for taking care of this puppy," she said. "She needs to be given food and water twice per day, played with, bathed, and has to go to the bathroom outside. She can sleep in a bed on the floor in your room. **Your first responsibility will be to name the puppy.**"

The Queen smiled at her daughters. *Oh, what fun they will have taking care of and playing with this puppy!* she thought.

The princess sisters walked away, with the little puppy following them. Princess Jenna picked her up.

"What do you think we should name her, Julia?"

"I think we should call her Rosie," Julia replied, "since you found her in the rose bushes and she has a pink collar!"

"That's a great name!" Princess Jenna looked the puppy in her little face. "Okay, puppy, we're going to call you Rosie. What do you think of that, Rosie?"

Rosie licked Princess Jenna's nose and wagged her tail.

"I think she likes it!" Princess Julia exclaimed.

The princess sisters took Rosie outside and let her run around the castle grounds. She barked at passing butterflies and chased her own tail, making the princesses laugh. As each day passed, Rosie seemed more and more comfortable with the princess sisters, and the princess sisters loved taking care of Rosie.

When it was time for dinner, the sisters and Rosie went into the castle's dining room. Princess Julia set out a bowl and filled it with water. Princess Jenna set out another bowl and filled it with chicken, green beans, and macaroni.

"No, no!" the King laughed. "Puppies don't eat people food, they eat dog food! Here, fill her bowl with this." The King passed Princess Jenna a bag of dog food. They all sat down at the table and began to eat, and so it became a tradition that every time the royal family ate together, Rosie ate right along with them.

One day, the princesses took Rosie to play outside after a rainy morning. Rosie jumped right into a muddy puddle and started to whimper. "Oh no," Princess Jenna said, "Rosie is sad she's all dirty! Her white fur is all brown. We should take her inside to give her a bath." Princess Julia picked her up and carried her inside. Princess Jenna filled the tub with warm water and found puppy shampoo. Princess Julia set Rosie into the bathtub. Rosie started running in the bathtub, trying to get out! The princesses quickly realized that Rosie did not like being wet either. They washed her as quickly as they could and tried to dry her off with a towel. Rosie wiggled away and ran all over the castle to dry off! She made everyone laugh.

At first, Rosie would sleep in her dog bed on the floor, between the two princesses' beds. One night, Rosie hopped on Princess Jenna's bed in the middle of the night. Princess Jenna woke up. "Oh, Rosie, you scared me! Are you cold?"

Rosie snuggled under the covers with Princess Jenna and rested her little fluffy head on her pillow. Princess Jenna and Rosie have slept like that every night since.

As the year passed on, the royal family celebrated all of the holidays and seasons with Rosie. They dressed Rosie up as a tiny giraffe for Halloween. They made Rosie a tiny pink jacket when it got chilly outside. The princesses made sure to give Rosie a Christmas present for her to open on Christmas morning. Rosie loved ripping the wrapping paper and finding a new toy! Rosie was really becoming part of their family.

One night, Princess Julia seemed sad. "What's the matter, honey?" the Queen asked Julia. "You've seemed sad all day. You didn't even laugh that hard when Rosie tried to climb the tree to chase the big green bird!"

"I am a little sad," sighed Princess Julia. "I just love Rosie so much, but I'm sad she's not officially a part of our family."

"Yeah, I agree," piped in Princess Jenna. "How do we make Rosie an official family member? I want Rosie to know that we're her proper family."

The Queen thought for a moment. Finally, she said, "Well, why don't we have a little royal ceremony to officially change Rosie's name to Princess Rosie? That way she'll be a real part of the royal family."

Princess Julia and Princess Jenna shouted with joy. They loved that idea!

The next week, the royal family had the ceremony.

The princess sisters gave Rosie a bath, which she did not like, but they wanted her to look her best. They made a new pink collar that read "Princess Rosie" and attached a little pink and gold cape to it.

The King led the ceremony. "Today, I, the King of the Land of Enchanted Forests, hereby declare that this white fluffy puppy named Rosie is officially a member of the royal family," he announced. "From this point forward, her official name will be Princess Rosie of the Land of Enchanted Forests!"

The King leaned forward to pet Rosie and give her a dog treat. The King placed a tiny soft crown on her head. Rosie wagged her tail and barked, and the princess sisters cheered. Rosie was officially a princess!

Princess Rosie had the best days playing outside with the princess sisters, chasing birds and bunnies, and trying to avoid bath time at all costs. Princess Rosie especially loved sleeping in Princess Jenna's bed every night. The princess sisters were so happy they had found Princess Rosie in the forest so long ago.

The princess sisters and the princess puppy were all best friends, and they lived happily ever after.

The End.

About the Author

Kristin Sponaugle was born in Butler, Pennsylvania. She graduated from Duquesne University, where she received her bachelor's degree in health sciences and her master's degree in physician assistant studies. Kristin had always dreamed of becoming an author, and made that dream a reality with her first published children's book, *The Princess Puppy*. In her spare time, she enjoys spending time with her husband, running, reading, cross-stitching, and playing with their Maltese dog, Rosie. Kristin lives with her husband and Rosie, and resides wherever the U.S. Air Force sends them.